For my parents — B.M.

For Tata — O.M.

Text copyright © 1996 by Barbara Maitland
Illustrations copyright © 1996 by Odilon Moraes
First American Edition 1997 published by Orchard Books
First published in Great Britain in 1996 by ABC, All Books for Children

Orchard Books
95 Madison Avenue
New York, NY 10016

Manufactured in Singapore
Book design by Anna Louise Billson

10 9 8 7 6 5 4 3 2 1

Library of Congress cataloging is available upon request.
ISBN 0-531-09546-0

The Bear Who Didn't Like HONEY

written by
Barbara Maitland

illustrated by
Odilon Moraes

ORCHARD BOOKS

NEW YORK

Little Bear didn't like the night.
He thought it was very dark.
   "I wasn't scared," said Little Bear.
"I just wasn't tired."
   "One night," said his father,
"you will sleep — all night long."
   But his brother and sisters said,
"Scaredy Bear! Scaredy Bear!"

And when it was time to fish,
the water looked very fast to Little Bear.
"I wasn't scared," said Little Bear.
"I was just cold."
"One day," said his mother,
"you will go in — all by yourself."
But his brother and sisters said,
"Scaredy Bear! Scaredy Bear!"

And when it was time to gather
honey from the nest near the cave, the
bees looked very dangerous to Little Bear.

"I wasn't scared," said Little Bear.
"I'm just not hungry."

"Never mind," said his father, "soon you —"

"No, he won't," interrupted his brother
and sisters. "He's Scaredy Bear, Scaredy Bear,"
they sang in a sticky chorus.

Little Bear heard a growl. Then he heard it again, only this time he felt it, too. It was his tummy! Little Bear *was* hungry. And that honey smelled better than salmon, better than nuts, better than berries. And he was sure it tasted better than anything he'd ever tasted.

"I am *not* Scaredy Bear!" he said. "I'm the Bear Who Doesn't Like Honey. I'll find something better."

And he set off
into the woods.
"Just be back
before it gets dark,"
said his mother.

Little Bear wasn't scared of the woods —
he often played in them. But he wondered
what he could find there that would be
better than honey.

"Hello," called a squirrel. "Who are you?"

"I'm the Bear Who Doesn't Like Honey."

"Unusual," said the squirrel.

"Hello," cheeped a bird. "Who are you?"
"I'm the Bear Who Doesn't Like Honey."
"A rare bear, indeed," said the bird.
Little Bear walked right past nuts,
and berries. He even walked right through
nap time. He was
a very hungry
bear now.

"Help!" he heard. "Help me, please!"

Little Bear looked up. He saw a tiny cub, smaller even than Little Bear, at the very top of a very tall tree, hanging on to a thin branch. It looked, thought Little Bear, as though it was about to snap right in half.

Little Bear knew he didn't have
time to go for help.

"I'm not scared," said Little Bear.
"I just don't like heights."

The cub's big eyes looked
right into Little Bear's.
Little Bear heard a whimper.

"I'm coming!" shouted Little Bear and, digging his claws deep into the bark of the tree, he climbed as fast as he could, right up to the top.

He reached out a paw, scooped up the cub, and bear-hugged his way back down while the cub clung to him.

Waiting at the bottom was a great big bear, smiling at him.

"Thank you for rescuing my cub," he said. "That was a very brave thing to do."

"It was?" asked Little Bear. "But I was scared!" And he began to cry.

"Sometimes," said the big bear, "we're all scared. What matters is that you tried. You did your best even though you were afraid, and that makes you a very brave bear."

Little Bear thought about what the big bear
had said, all the way home. When he reached
the edge of the woods, he saw the bees
buzzing around their nest. His tummy
rumbled and growled.

"Honey!" shouted Little Bear and,
with one huge swipe of his paw,
he captured a honeycomb.

"MMMmmm!" It was better than salmon,
better than nuts, better than berries, better
than anything he'd ever tasted before.
And it was better than any other
honey because he'd got it
all by himself.

Little Bear hurried into the cave where his parents were waiting for him. "It turns out," he said, licking his paws, "that I'm a Bear Who Does Like Honey after all."

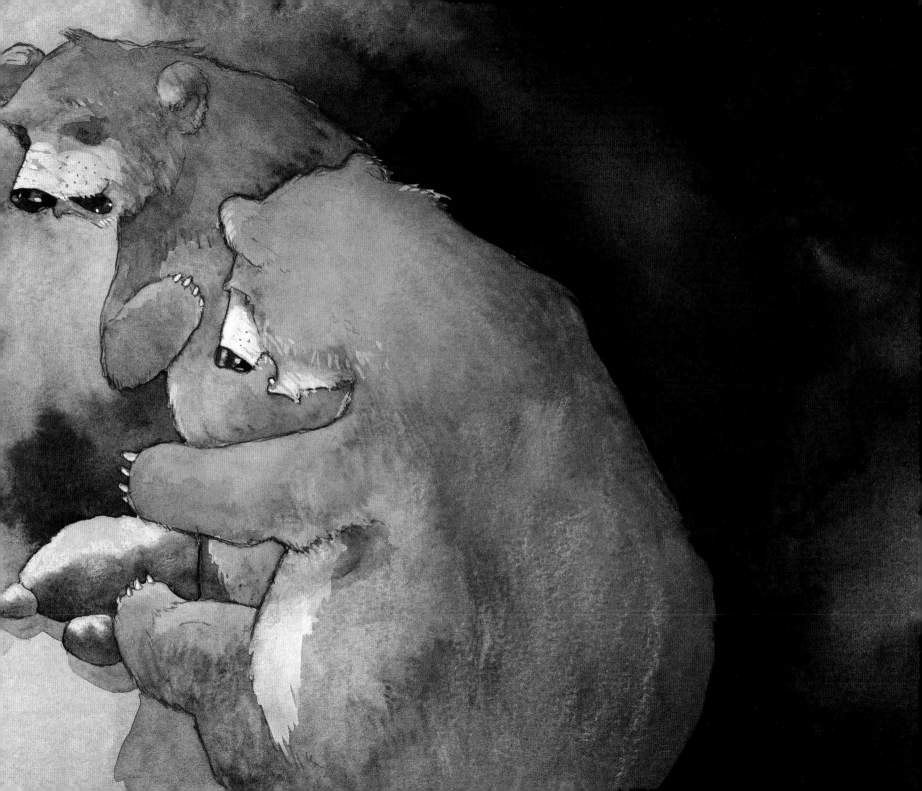

Then he snuggled up next to
his brother and sisters and slept —
all night long.